Postman Pat
Goes Sledging

Story by **John Cunliffe** *Pictures by* **Celia Berridge**

from the original Television designs by **Ivor Wood**

Hippo Books
Scholastic Publications Limited
London

Scholastic Publications Ltd.,
10 Earlham Street, London WC2H 9LN

Scholastic Inc.,
730 Broadway, New York, NY 10003, USA

Scholastic Tab Publications Ltd.,
123 Newkirk Road,
Richmond Hill,
Ontario L4C 3G5, Canada

Ashton Scholastic Pty Ltd.,
PO Box 579, Gosford, New South Wales,
Australia

Ashton Scholastic Ltd., 165 Marua Road,
Panmure, Auckland 6, New Zealand

First published by Andre Deutsch, 1984

Published in paperback by Scholastic Publications Ltd., 1985
Text copyright © 1984 John Cunliffe
Illustrations © 1984 Celia Berridge and Ivor Wood
ISBN 0 590 70417 6
All rights reserved
Made and Printed by Mateu Cromo, Madrid
Typeset in Plantin

There was deep snow in Greendale.

Peter Fogg was out early. He had the snow-plough fitted to the big tractor, and he was clearing the snow from the roads. No one could get about until the roads were cleared, and the council snow-plough would be busy on the main roads around Pencaster.

Peter left a clear way behind him, and a little procession followed . . . .
Postman Pat in his van;
Sam Waldron in his mobile-shop;
and Miss Hubbard on her bike.

The Reverend Timms was digging the snow from the vicarage path, and waved as they all went by.

At the village post-office, Mrs. Goggins was full of news.

"They do say there are ten-foot drifts up the top road, Pat, and here's an urgent parcel for George Lancaster. You'll never get up there to-day, you know, not with all this snow."

"Oh dear," said Pat, "but I'd better take it, just in case I can get through. I usually manage, somehow."

"Well, mind how you go, Pat. We don't want you getting buried in the snow like those poor sheep."

"Oh, I'll be all right. Cheerio!"

Pat was on his way, driving slowly along the slippery roads.

At Greendale Farm, the twins were waiting for Pat, with a pile of
snowballs. A snowball whizzed through the air, and hit Pat right on the nose.
"Oh, you young monkeys!" shouted Pat. "Two can play at that game."

He made a big snowball, and aimed at Tom's nose.
"Oh!"
Oh dear! Tom dodged. Pat was not a good shot and, just at that moment,
Alf Thompson came out of the house. *Smack!* The snowball hit him right in
the face.
"Oh, sorry, Mr. Thompson!" shouted Pat, "I didn't know you were there.
I was aiming at the twins."

"That's all right," said Alf. "It's only a bit of fun. Now then, Pat, you'll have to stop here a bit. The road's blocked and Peter's stuck with his tractor in a big drift. We've come to try and dig it out. Can you give us a hand?"

"Certainly," said Pat.

He gave Mrs. Pottage her letters. Then he borrowed a spade and set out along the snowy road with Alf and Ted Glen. When they came to the tractor, Peter was already hard at work, digging out the high wall of snow.

They all joined in. It took a long time to make a big enough gap. Then Peter started up the tractor and took a run at the snowdrift.

"Hurrah!" He was through.

Pat, Ted and Alf walked back to Greendale Farm. The twins had been busy, too. They had built a snowman.

Now Pat's van could get through, so off he went. He called at the vicarage with letters for the Reverend Timms, but Dr. Gilbertson came to the door.

"Come in, Pat," she said. "The Reverend's slipped on the ice and broken his leg. I've just finished bandaging him up. The ambulance will be coming for him, as soon as the roads are clear."

There was the Reverend, sitting with his leg propped up on a cushion, in splints and bandages. He cheered up when he saw Pat with his letters.

"Wasn't this a silly thing to do, Pat," he said. "And I was just going to take the parish magazine round too. *Now* what am I going to do?"

"Don't worry," said Pat. "I can take it with my letters. No trouble at all. I'll see they get through. Now you enjoy your letters, and rest that leg, and you'll soon be better. Cheerio!"

At Thompson Ground, Dorothy Thompson was out collecting the eggs. "I hope you haven't any letters for anybody up the top road," she said.

"The snow's so bad that Peter had to turn back. The tractor just couldn't get up the hill. It was slipping all over the place."

"Well, yes, I have a parcel for George, and it's marked URGENT," said Pat. "What can I do? Perhaps I could walk it?"

"I have a better idea," said Alf. "We can go up on the old farm sledge. I have to take some food up for the sheep, anyway."

"Well.... it's a long time since I was on a sledge," said Pat doubtfully. Alf pulled the big sledge out of the barn.

"Here we are," he said, "we'll be all right on this."

"And you'd better take George some groceries," said Dorothy. "He'll be getting short, with being snowed up. Jess can stay by the fire, with me."

They loaded the sledge up, with bales of hay and a box of groceries, and off they went.

It was hard going uphill. Alf pulled and Pat pushed. When they came to a downhill stretch, they jumped on and rode, skimming over the frozen snow. That was *lovely!*

Alf's sheep were glad to see them. They gathered round in the snow, bleating. Alf untied the bales of hay, and spread the hay on the snow. The sheep ran to it with little bleats of joy. Then Alf and Pat pushed on to Intake Farm.

George's house was half buried in the snow. Pat knocked at the door.
"Hello!" he called. "Anybody in?"
There was no answer.
"George'll be out, seeing to *his* sheep," said Alf. "The door's sure to be open."
It was, so they left the parcel and the box of groceries on the kitchen table, with a note, on the back of an old envelope.

Now the sledge was empty, and it was downhill most of the way back.
"We'll have a fast ride home," said Alf. "Hold tight, Pat! Give us a push!
Here we go!"
And off they went.

They whizzed across the fields, faster and faster. The snow was so deep that they went over the tops of the walls. They hit a bump, and over they went, tumbled and rolled in a deep drift of snow. They picked themselves up, found the sledge, climbed aboard, and off they went again. Pat hadn't enjoyed himself so much for years. Faster and faster, down the hill they went.

"How are we going to stop?" Pat shouted.

"I don't know!" shouted Alf. "Just hang on!"

Alf had forgotten how to stop a sledge, but they soon found out! Thompson Ground came into sight, and Alf steered for the yard.

They shot through the open gate, scattering hens in all directions, and straight into the barn. They crashed into a pile of hay bales, and fell off again, shouting and laughing. What a mess they were! They were covered in snow, bits of hay, and muck from the barn floor. They staggered into the house like drunken scarecrows.

Jess was curled up on the rug in front of a warm fire. Dorothy had the kettle on. Alf and Pat cleaned themselves up, warmed themselves by the fire, and soon had a good hot mug of tea in their hands.

"My goodness – that *was* an exciting ride," said Pat. "But I'd better be on my way now. I still have some letters to deliver. Thanks for the ride and the tea. Come on, Jess, you'll have to leave that fire, now. Cheerio!"

The rest of Pat's round was in the valley, and the roads had been cleared
and gritted by now.

"No more digging or sledging to-day," said Pat to Jess. "It'll take more than
snow to stop us."

But Jess was curled up, fast asleep, and dreaming of that lovely warm
fireside and Mrs. Thompson's woolly rug.